FIVE GO PARENTING

Other adventures in this series:

Five Go Gluten Free
Five Go on a Strategy Away Day
Five on Brexit Island
Five Give Up the Booze

Enid Blyton

FIVE GO
PARENTING

Text by
Bruno Vincent

Enid Blyton for Grown-Ups

Quercus

First published in Great Britain in 2016 by

Quercus Editions Ltd
Carmelite House
50 Victoria Embankment
London EC4Y 0DZ

An Hachette UK company

A CIP catalogue record for this book is available
from the British Library

HB ISBN 978 1 78648 228 0
EBOOK ISBN 978 1 78648 229 7

Text by Bruno Vincent
Original illustrations by Eileen A. Soper
Cover illustration by Ruth Palmer

10 9 8 7 6 5 4 3 2 1

Typeset by CC Book Production

Printed and bound in Great Britain by Clays Ltd, St Ives plc

Contents

CHAPTER ONE

A Daring Escape

Dick and Julian crept along the dark corridor in silence. They peered into the gloom, trying to make out the objects around them, desperate not to make a noise. Each footfall was a slow, delicate manoeuvre, and they moved with the careful deliberation of a pair of astronauts on a moonwalk.

Now they had made their bid for liberation, darkness was their friend. There was no going back, and if they were caught, the consequences would be dire. But the front door was only a few feet away, and beyond that, freedom. They hardly dared to breathe.

Dick reached out slowly to grasp the handle. He turned cautiously to see if Julian was in step behind him. They gave each other a thumbs-up. Although he could hardly make out Julian's face in the darkness, Dick was mystified as he thought he saw Julian's features distort into agony.

Julian thrust a hand up to cover his mouth but it was too late. A shout of pain had escaped, which must have been audible

Wendy stood up, carefully adjusted the blanket, and held the carrier in front of Dick so he could see what was inside.

for miles. And from nearby the alarm went up – a familiar loud wailing that struck a chill into their hearts.

Ahead of them, a door opened wide and a manly shape filled it, with hands on hips.

'Oh, *fiddlesticks*,' said Dick, as the light was switched on.

'What the hell is this noise?' asked George angrily.

'I trod on a plastic toy swan,' said Julian. 'I think I'm bleeding!'

'Well, congratulations, you pair of utter arse-clowns,' she said. 'You've woken her up. Where did you think you were going?'

'We were just briefly nipping out for a quick pint,' said Dick meekly.

Anne came into the corridor, holding the baby, making reassuring noises.

'Who knows how long it will take to get her back to sleep?' She tutted over her shoulder at her brothers.

'So, just to be clear, we *can't* go out to the pub, then?' asked Dick. 'Or can we?'

'*Just to be clear*,' said Anne sharply, 'for the foreseeable future, *none* of us will be going anywhere *near* a pub.'

Dick and Julian gaped at each other. Here was a horror that went beyond human understanding.

CHAPTER TWO

An Adventure Comes to a Happy Resolution

Six Days Earlier.

'Thanks to you youngsters,' said the rotund policeman, 'these troublemakers will be out of mischief for many years to come!'

Julian, Anne, Dick and George beamed with pride.

'Woof!' said Timmy enthusiastically.

They were all standing in a dimly lit warehouse in Whitechapel, watching as their dastardly cousin Rupert and his Eastern-European wife were being led away in handcuffs. Ordinarily, they would expect someone they had just captured to snarl at them bitterly and promise a bloodcurdling revenge, but these two remained silent and composed as they were walked towards separate police cars. Perhaps they were already thinking about their defence.

'Just how did you know they would be here with the illegal shipment at this precise moment?' said the policeman in wonder. 'It beggars belief!'

'I'm glad you asked,' said Anne, excitedly. 'I was first made

4

suspicious when I saw that the "iPhones" Rupert had been importing arrived in boxes from North K—'

'I haven't actually got time to listen to your explanation right now,' said the policeman. 'I've got a warehouse of evidence to log. We'll need to fix up for you to come into the station and give a full written statement later in the week.'

'Oh,' said Julian.

'In the past,' said Dick, 'we were always sort of patted on the head, and then left to our own devices.'

'Yes, well, that was the past. Right now, if you wouldn't mind vacating the crime scene, PC Difford will take your details and show you out. If you ask nicely, she might pat you on the head.'

The five of them wandered towards the exit with a slight feeling of anticlimax. Stepping out into the moonlight, they checked their phones.

'It's the middle of the night,' said Julian. 'Tubes aren't even running yet.'

'I've called an Uber,' said George, pocketing her phone. 'It will be here in five.'

'I say, Anne,' said Dick, eager for his dear younger sister not to miss out on her chance to shine, 'that was terribly clever of you to think of coming here, and to find your way into the warehouse all by yourself. Was it a secret passage that you discovered?'

A third bag contained a bucket-sized tub of nappy-rash cream, ear plugs, bottles, a pot of formula and a breast pump.

'No,' said Anne thoughtfully. 'It usually is, but not this time . . .'

'He will now be here in eight,' said George, checking her phone and frowning. 'He's driving a silver Prius.'

CHAPTER THREE

A Terrible Surprise

After breakfast the next day, the housemates found themselves at a bit of a loose end. As fresh-faced youths, foiling an evil plot had always been followed by treats and attention from adults. Now they were adults themselves, it was different. No one seemed to give much of a monkey's. Perhaps, in the old days, they would have gone off into the countryside together. But there wasn't much countryside to go off into in this part of north London. And besides, there was rain forecast for later.

Dick suggested a cycle ride, but George's bike had a puncture and Julian, who didn't have one, refused to hire 'one of those rotten Boris bikes' because he considered them part of a 'socialist plot'. Julian's politics could sometimes be a bit hard to pin down. Announcing he had some work to do, he wandered into his bedroom.

Dick watched *Match of the Day 2* on iPlayer while Anne sat on the armchair, legs tucked under her, knitting a tea cosy in the pattern of the cover artwork to Radiohead's most recent album (a birthday present for Julian, bringing together two of his favourite things). George was on her laptop.

A fly buzzed peacefully through the room.

'Shall we have a curry tonight?' Dick asked suddenly.

'We've got leftovers,' said Anne, without looking up.

'I feel as though we should do something to celebrate,' Dick said.

'Fine, I'll throw the leftovers away,' said Anne quietly.

There was an awkward pause, and then Dick blew a raspberry. 'You worry too much,' he said. 'They'll keep for another day.'

George closed her laptop, looked at her nails, then looked out of the window. She burped.

'Okay, I'm officially bored,' she said.

The doorbell rang.

All of them leapt up to answer it, Julian even coming out of his room. They all secretly hoped this would be news of some unfinished aspect of the adventure that would need their attention. Perhaps Cousin Rupert still had associates on the run. Perhaps he had anticipated their meddling and had planted an explosive device in their flat as revenge. *Gosh*, that would be exciting.

They all reached the door simultaneously, and Anne opened it.

Desperate not to make a noise, each footfall was a slow,
delicate manoeuvre, and they moved with the careful
deliberation of a pair of astronauts on a moonwalk.

A TERRIBLE SURPRISE

On their doorstep stood a pleasant-looking middle-aged lady in a business suit. In her right hand she was holding a baby carrier.

'I'm from social services,' she said, smiling. 'My name is Wendy.'

'Right,' said Anne. 'Well, I'll see what I've got in my purse . . .'

'Oh, *Anne*,' said George crossly.

'Social services is a part of the government,' the woman said. 'We don't canvass door-to-door for donations. That comes from your taxes.'

'I'll say it does,' said Julian.

'Won't you come in?' Anne asked, eager to change the conversation.

'Thank you,' said the lady. 'She's sleeping,' she added quietly, placing the baby carrier on the table.

While they all wondered what this woman could possibly be doing here with a baby, Dick offered her tea or coffee. She gratefully accepted a cup of tea.

'Now,' she said. 'I understand that you are related to Lily Mackenzie Kapulsky Kirrin?'

The four young people on the other side of the table breathed a unanimous sigh of relief.

'No,' Julian said. 'Definitely not.'

'Unless she's some distant aunt we've never heard of before,' said George with a thrill in her voice, 'and has left us an unimaginable fortune?'

'In which case, we definitely are,' said Julian, 'and will somehow prove it.'

'Because Kirrin *is* our surname, you see,' said Anne. 'But we've never heard of this person; I'm sorry.'

This was all going wrong – Wendy shut her eyes and shook her head violently, as though to shake the conversation to pieces, so she could start again. 'Let me put it like this,' she said. 'Are you the next of kin for Rupert and Anastasia Kirrin?'

They all stared at her for a moment.

'I suppose we *could* be,' said Julian. 'I certainly know that Rupert is an only child, and his mother – his last remaining parent – only recently passed away.'

'Well then, perhaps you know the child by a nickname?'

Their expressions somehow managed to grow even blanker than before.

'Hopefully this won't come as too much of a shock,' said Wendy, battling on. 'I'm sure you appreciate that, where possible, it's best to avoid putting children into foster care. It's far better for the child to be with the family. I see . . .' She faltered. 'I see that this *is* perhaps a bit of a surprise . . .'

As the implication of what Wendy was trying to say dawned

on them, Julian, Anne and George all blanched, as though the woman in front of them had transmogrified into a terrifying ghoul. Then, slowly and with equal horror, their eyes slid towards the baby carrier.

Only Dick continued smiling, unperturbed. Wendy decided to focus on him for the moment.

'It seems you did know about this?' she asked him.

'Oh, no,' Dick said pleasantly. 'I'm afraid I haven't the faintest idea what you're talking about.'

Wendy stood up, carefully adjusted the blanket, and held the carrier in front of Dick so he could see what was inside.

Dick screamed as he had never screamed before.

CHAPTER FOUR

Taking Responsibility

About half an hour later, Wendy (who told them she was a mum to four of her own) had succeeded in calming the baby down enough that she finally lulled somewhere close to sleep.

Julian, George and Anne had also just about succeeded in calming Dick down, through a combination of large glasses of brandy and slaps to the face. He was now sitting back at the table, looking tired and woozy.

The others were not exactly calm themselves, for, if Wendy was going where they thought she was going with this, it was the biggest bombshell that could possibly have gone off in their lives.

At last, Wendy sat opposite and resumed where she had left off. It became immediately apparent that she was going precisely where they had feared.

'Now, you may well feel that you are unequal to this task, and in response I would say that, if you want to give her up for fostering or adoption, that is entirely up to you. The correct procedures will be gone through. But, for the time being, of

*They rapidly learned that all parenting literature fell into
two opposing camps. Both sounded utterly convincing.*

course, her family status is up in the air. Her parents will be tried in a criminal court, which might take months (years, conceivably) to come to a conclusion. In this part of a child's life, it is absolutely crucial for her to be with family members who love her and can provide essential, nourishing, emotional care.' She looked them all over, and was impressed by the gravity with which they had taken in her words. 'I see you all understand this.'

They would perhaps have chosen the word 'panic' as an emotional keynote at that moment, but, one by one, they met her eye and nodded.

'That's good,' she said. 'Now, I'll need you to sign these forms . . .'

Within the hour, after the reading and signing (in quadruplicate) of a very large amount of paperwork, and with the promise to return soon and frequently, Wendy was gone. But Lily wasn't.

Wendy had left a bushel of advisory literature for them to plough through, and had told them what to do in the first few days: change her nappy, feed her bottles, and help her sleep.

The four of them stood over the basket while Timmy squirmed in and out of their legs, panting, aware that something exciting was occurring.

The baby was dozing, her eyes gently blinking open and

shut, unconsciously twiddling her fingers. She had a light dusting of blond hair that didn't quite cover her head yet. She looked entirely innocent and vulnerable, and this produced a sharp pain in the hearts of those who looked down on her.

Julian shut his eyes and grabbed on to Anne and George, to calm him down. 'Okay,' he said, breathing deeply, looking at the ceiling. 'Okay. Okay, this is actually happening. Oh, shit.'

'So Cousin Rupert had a baby!' said Anne. 'We have a cousin!'

'I really wish we had known that before we had him sent to prison,' said Dick.

'Oh, you'd have let him off, would you?' asked Julian.

'Well . . .' Dick thought. 'No, but we could have just given him a rap on the knuckles, you know? Warned him to stop his activities.'

'Why didn't they *let us know*?' Anne asked.

'Anne, you're right,' George said. 'You're the real victim here.'

'It seems sort of unfair,' said Dick. 'On her, I mean. I've never even *thought* about looking after a baby. Not once. It's like forcing a blind man to be a bus driver.'

'We'll muddle through,' said Anne uncertainly. She sniffed

the air, then sniffed again, closer to the baby. 'Oh dear. We have a situation.'

She looked at the others, and the others looked at her.

'Are you bored now, George?' she asked.

'No,' George conceded, shaking her head. 'No, I am not.'

CHAPTER FIVE

The Nappy Question

They went to investigate the bags that had been left. Wendy had brought over all she could reclaim from Rupert's house and fit in her car. This included a big bag of baby clothes and a box of toys – including, most importantly, Sophie the Giraffe, a teething toy. Sophie's poor squishy head spent all waking hours in Lily's mouth, being gummed out of shape.

A third bag contained sundries, including a bucket-sized tub of nappy-rash cream, ear plugs, plastic crockery and cutlery, bottles, a pot of formula and a breast pump – which Dick played with, chuckling, until he was told what it was, when he dropped and broke it.

'No loss,' said Julian. 'We couldn't use it, anyway, unless we found a cow . . .'

'Ah! Here we are,' said Anne, finding a bag full of nappies.

'So . . . Who goes first?' asked George.

'I don't think it's decent for it to be me who does that,' said Julian.

'Come on, Jules,' said Dick. 'You don't think that's really

They had known, intellectually, that she would cry. But they could not have prepared for how much or how violently.

going to work, do you? Be brave and move forward into the 1970s.'

Dick so rarely spoke back to Julian that he couldn't think of anything to say in response.

'This is new for everyone,' said George. 'We'll have to take it in turns. Doesn't matter who goes first. I'll do it.' She looked down and saw that little Lily was alive, and awake. Taking a deep breath, she reached into the carrycot and picked her up by the armpits. She held Lily out to the others. Roused from her slumber, Lily looked at them.

'Well, hello there,' said Dick, shaking her little hand. Lily grabbed his forefinger and squeezed. And, in so doing, wrapped her tiny fingers around his heart. 'Aren't you delightful,' he said, in a much gentler voice.

'I suppose we did put her parents in prison,' said Anne. 'We've brought this on ourselves.'

Anne took Lily while George spread a cloth on the table and put the nappies and wet wipes down on it.

'You're not going to do it there, are you?' said Julian. 'We're going to eat off that later.'

'Fine, I'll do it on the floor,' said George. 'And there's no use slinking off; it'll be your turn soon. You might as well watch.'

Julian, Dick and Anne all accepted their fate grimly. Their

expressions did not alter much as George progressed with the deed, and, if anything, deepened.

First, George detached the fastenings of the old nappy, which she then carefully unfolded from the baby. Lily's entire body beneath her belly button looked like it had been dipped in satay sauce. Somehow, the mess had spread everywhere with exact evenness. George folded the spent nappy quickly and placed it aside, but it seemed, even there, she made a mistake, because oblivious Lily explored her newfound freedom by wriggling and squirming and twisting around.

George yelped and grabbed a baby wipe, then gently tried to hold Lily in place while she cleaned the besmeared areas of skin. However, whichever part she cleaned, it rubbed straight away against a dirty part, and Lily (who had no expression except for intense thoughtfulness) danced and wriggled, and at one point actually started spinning. Eventually, by moving her to a fresh corner of changing mat, and moving with an intense, almost frantic speed, George managed to get clean, all at the same time, a large number of the contaminating areas: hands, arms, knees, thighs and feet. This achieved, she lost no time in mopping up all the other places too.

Throughout, the other three offered a constant stream of advice that in any other activity would have qualified as infuriating backseat driving. But George needed all the help she could get, and was grateful for the many mutterings of 'You've missed a bit there'. After all, this wasn't a task at which you could admit defeat and give up. It simply had to be done.

When Lily was finally and incontrovertibly clean, there was a round of applause, which George, red faced and puffing, accepted with a reluctant smile.

'Hand me a new one, then,' she said. As a nappy was passed

'Just to be clear,' said Anne sharply, 'for the foreseeable future none of us will be going anywhere near a pub.'

into her hand, she turned back to Lily, trying to locate in her mind what that odd noise was that she had just heard. It sounded rather like a wet towel slapping on a marble floor, or a bubble rising lazily through cooling magma.

The applause stopped at once.

'Good Lord,' said Dick. 'I didn't know they could do that!'

'My bloody bookshelf!' said Julian. 'My Wodehouse hard-backs!'

'I'll fetch a cloth,' said Anne, seeing this was not a task for baby wipes.

It was perhaps good for the housemates to learn so many lessons in one: that a recently soiled nappy was no assurance that a baby wasn't ready to go again; that you must get the nappy on as fast as possible after the previous one comes off, during which time precious moments could be wasted trying to work out which way round it went; and that the blast range of liquid baby poo was both dangerous and strangely impressive. (Anne did, thankfully, succeed in getting Lily's effluent off Julian's P. G. Wodehouse hardbacks – a miraculous effort, as initially the shelf had looked like the target at a paintballing contest.)

The whole experience had been like trying to put trousers on a distracted octopus, and it was agreed that the task would be best performed in twos for the foreseeable future. When

Lily was in comfy dry clothes again, Dick prepared a bottle for her and Julian made them all a cup of tea. George sat, looking harrowed, while Anne did some calculations about the number of bottles Lily needed a day, the number they had, and therefore how many needed to be sterilized at any one time. She chewed the pen as she made this calculation, then put a rota on the little kitchen whiteboard where they normally left shopping lists.

'So this is our life now, is it?' asked George.

'Come on,' said Dick. 'We always throw ourselves into any new adventure, heart and soul. This is no different! Lily has come to us because we did the Right Thing. Now we're custodians to a human life. And so we'll do the Right Thing again.'

'She said it might take years,' said Julian, passing out the cups and tipping some fruit shortcake biscuits on to a plate.

'There's no sense worrying about it,' said Dick. 'Look.' He bent down and picked Lily up, then sat her on the table in front of him, so she was looking at the others. He gave her his finger and she grabbed it again, and squeezed. For some reason, despite the fact it made the bottom of his stomach fall away, this was the most wonderfully gratifying and reassuring sensation he thought he'd ever felt.

George looked round distractedly and was surprised to find

Lily staring candidly back at her. Lily's eyes were a remarkably intense blue. Her cheeks and neck, her hands and arms were all so pale and plump, they seemed edible. She waved her arms around until, by sheer coincidence, she slapped her palms together. She blinked with surprise, tried to do it again. Second time, she missed, but the third time she made contact again. She made a gurgling noise, and smiled.

At the sight of this smile, Julian, George and Anne all put their mugs down, forgetting their thirst at once. Their chairs screeched as they moved closer to Dick, and half an hour disappeared as they played with Lily, and kissed her, and cuddled her, and asked her rhetorical questions in high-pitched voices.

They were in love.

Everything had changed.

Timmy watched, panting, fascinated.

CHAPTER SIX

Getting Used to the New Family Member

The first issue was where to put her. They initially set the cot up in the living room, but it quickly seemed like madness to try this long-term and so Dick's room was chosen, with Dick, for the time being, sleeping on the sofa.

That evening, after sleeping for an hour or so, Lily woke up and cried. Despite having her own room, her cries were audible from every corner of the flat.

They all sprang into action. They walked her around and they sang to her; they leant her on their shoulders and bounced her on their knees; they rocked her gently, making cooing noises. Hours passed, but still Lily wailed inconsolably.

They had known, intellectually, that she would cry. But they could not have prepared for how much or how violently. It was very hard to tell what she was crying about, if anything.

'This is no good,' said Julian, after she had been going six hours. 'We need to do research, and we need to sleep. Let's split into teams.'

So they did. George and Dick tried to sleep, while the other two alternated looking after baby Lily and absorbing all the parenting literature they could find. They rapidly learnt that all parenting literature fell strictly into one of two opposing camps. Both sounded absolutely convincing.

One said you must respond to crying at once, find out by a process of elimination what it was that the baby was unhappy about, and tend to this need until it was resolved. This seemed the natural human approach. The other said that you should let the baby cry until it got used to the rhythms you enforced upon it, whereafter both baby and parents would thrive happily with a structured lifestyle. This seemed the intelligent, informed approach.

As they would find in the ensuing weeks, neither approach was possible to follow rigorously, the first for practical reasons and the second for emotional ones – specifically, the relentless emotional attrition caused by the wailing of an unattended baby. Many discussions followed, but no conclusion could be reached about which was the best method – and so they employed a hodgepodge that would have disappointed or horrified the advocates of either.

At the end of each shift, they switched. Except for occasional twenty- or thirty-minute bouts of comatose exhaustion, Lily remained stubbornly awake almost constantly, for the majority of which time she was crying.

'I feel as though crying this much ought to diminish the power of crying,' said Dick. 'Like getting used to the sound of a motorway if you live right next to it. But somehow it doesn't. She looks so miserable.'

'We'll get the hang of it,' said Julian. 'There has to be a knack to this parenting lark.' But despite his jolly words, his cheeks were hollow and his eyes were empty.

'It's funny you say that,' said George, 'because I feel literally useless. I have no idea what I'm doing. It's like one of those dreams where you find yourself on stage at the opera. Except it's real, and never-ending.'

'Come on,' said Anne, hoisting Lily on her lap and wiping away the tears and snot. 'We've never failed on an adventure before. There will be a way through this, and we'll find it. Won't we, darling Lily? Dearest little girl?' she asked the baby, who smiled at her with her big eyes and mashed her lips as she sicked up an ounce of yellow gunk.

Lily proved to have no respect for bedtimes – or any civilized hours, in fact.

'She has to sleep soon,' said Julian that night. 'It stands to

29

'We'll get the hang of it,' said Julian. 'There has to be a trick to this parenting lark.' But despite his jolly words, his cheeks were hollow and his eyes were empty.

reason. She just can't have that much energy. If I cried that much, I'd go into a coma.'

'I don't see what she's got to moan about,' said Dick.

'Without having any choice, she's been born into a huge indifferent universe that will slowly crush her spirit, and then she will die,' said George. 'I'm on her side. Crying's the least she could do.'

'George,' said Anne reprovingly, 'she's not old enough to

have object permanence, so she *definitely* doesn't have existential angst.'

'Well, I bloody have,' said George.

'Me too,' Julian admitted. 'This isn't working. I feel like I've been turned inside out. There has to be some solution!'

'Woof!' agreed Timmy mournfully.

CHAPTER SEVEN

Soothing Songs for Baby

The constant and overwhelming feeling they all had was that they had no idea what they were doing, and they should not be allowed to take care of this child.

All four of them suffered the agonizing fear, whenever they stood up with Lily in their arms, that (lightheaded with sleep deprivation as they were, and with spots of sick and spilled food on the floor) they would trip and fall at any moment, and commit murder. She was, after all, so *light*, and so delicate. However, they couldn't admit such dark thoughts out loud and so each of them thought they were the only one plagued with this (universal) dread.

One of the only palliative treatments for Awful Terrible Intense Crying, which is what George had dubbed the disease young Lily was suffering from, was singing to her while she was strapped to one's chest in a sling. The sound, the proximal warmth and the gentle movement often persuaded her to leave off crying quite so hard, and relax into a sort of keening moan. And, occasionally, to descend into a few minutes of light snoozing.

In the first week she was in their care, Dick slowly learnt to do many things while singing with Lily strapped to his chest. These included cutting his toenails, microwaving a burrito, doing his online banking and unblocking the toilet. In fact, despite the occasional mishap, like spitting toothpaste on to her head rather than into the basin, he began to feel rather good at it.

He sang 'The Wheels on the Bus' to her while he played *Gears of War* online; he sang 'Row, Row, Row Your Boat' while he updated his CV (unwittingly listing one of his hobbies as 'playing tennis gently down the stream'). He sang and sang and sang, and the songs stopped being songs, and became mantras.

The others admired Dick for his instinctive skill at this – none of them could replicate it. When it came their turn to care for Lily, perhaps because they lacked Dick's uncomplicated sunniness, they struggled to achieve the same results. Only Timmy could calm her half as well as Dick did. The spectacle of his enormous panting head and great lolling tongue was something that fascinated Lily – and, for his part, Timmy loved her too, offering many a friendly lick that elicited smiles and gurgling laughs.

In their efforts to make Lily sleep, therefore, the others turned to music for assistance.

Julian naturally tended towards something educational and improving, and didn't see why classical music would not be soothing for a child. He started with things that were beautiful and gentle: Mozart's Horn Concerto, Handel's *Water Music*, Tchaikovsky's *Swan Lake* and Erik Satie's *Gymnopédies* and *Gnossiennes*. Listening to them while Lily cried did make him feel slightly better, but didn't seem to improve her mood very much. At the end of his shift, he decided to rethink his approach and plan his next move.

Anne replaced him. She held poor wakeful Lily against her shoulder and murmured softly, walking up and down, up and down. She put her disc into the player, ejecting Julian's Erik Satie CD with a tut and a sigh. She had prepared a mix-tape disc of tunes from the American songbook: beautiful, gentle love songs by Gershwin and Cole Porter.

Like Julian, she found it easier to put up with the crying while listening to some of her favourite tracks. Even when mixed with the moaning of an unhappy child, Anne's heart was lifted by the elegance of 'Somethin' Stupid', 'Smoke Gets in Your Eyes', 'I Got Rhythm' and 'I've Got You Under My Skin'. She sang along gently, rubbing Lily's back, and even felt her own eyes prick with tears at times.

But the CD came to an end and, a while later, so did Anne's shift. If challenged, she would have admitted her meticulously

*George sat looking harrowed while Anne did some
calculations about the number of bottles Lily needed a day.*

crafted playlist had not made a noticeable impression on Lily's sleeplessness. She, too, retired thoughtfully to consider what to do next time.

George replaced her. She noticed the tossed-aside Satie CD, which she recognized as Julian's contribution. She chuckled to herself at his pretentiousness, but pocketed the disc, as she wanted to listen to it. She popped open the player to have a look at Anne's CD, raising an eyebrow at what seemed to her a noble effort. Shutting the lid again, George plugged her smartphone into the stereo and searched on the music app for her playlist. Lily was restless on her shoulder, tossing her head one way then another.

'Peace, child, peace,' George said, kissing and stroking the top of her head. 'Soon you shall be entertained. Now, check out this mutha.' She had already spent four fruitless and unhappy sessions trying to get Lily to sleep this week, and had come up with a plan. She pressed play.

It seemed to George (who would freely admit she was no expert) that very small children were insensible, impervious to taste, and responsive only to coarse sensation. In this, she reasoned, they were like grown-ups who bought novelty records. Therefore, why not appeal to that part of her brain?

Following this line of logic, George had prepared a CD of precisely the most gaudy and absurd tracks that adult music-lovers would do anything to avoid, which she now played at a low volume. It started modestly with 'Combine Harvester' by The Wurzels and 'I'm the Urban Spaceman' by The Bonzo Dog Doo-Dah Band. Then it stepped up a gear with 'Star Trekkin'' and 'Shaddap You Face' by Joe Dolce. After passing through various intermediate stages, the record crescendoed with the 'The Ketchup Song' by Las Ketchup.

During this, George danced around (as gently as possible), sang along, made faces and generally amused both herself and Lily. By the end of the final track, she was exhausted, but she and Lily had been having a jolly nice and silly time, and when she handed over to Dick, she felt she was giving him a baby far more likely to sleep than not.

Dick saw this in Lily's eyes when he took her, and, once George had departed, implemented his usual routine – but with one new, brilliant embellishment he had come up with in the intervening hours. He used both a CD *and* a smartphone. On the CD, he played the baby songs, and, out loud, he sang gently along with 'Sing a Song of Sixpence', 'Frère Jacques' and the like, as had become second nature to him. But, at the same time, he plugged his earphones in and pressed play on a video-games podcast he had downloaded. He was good to go for the next hour or two . . .

CHAPTER EIGHT

Some Visitors Come By

Within days, relatives descended upon them with advice and toys. Uncle Quentin and Aunt Fanny made a brief visit during which Uncle Quentin succeeded in remaining in the car outside, waving up at them from the driving seat, the motor still running.

'He's thinking about one of his science projects,' Aunt Fanny explained, after she had been introduced to the baby. 'Oh, *look*,' she said, pointing. They looked. Somehow Lily had managed to take one of her blocks and (presumably while trying to do something else, like throw it, or eat it) had balanced it on another. 'She's going to be an *engineer*!' said Aunt Fanny, clapping her hands.

'How does it feel to be Great Aunt Fanny?' asked Dick.

'I have always been great, Dick,' she said, 'as you well know.'

'She won't sleep, and she cries all the time,' said George. 'I think she might be mental.'

'Can someone pass me a clean muslin please? Quick?
Thank you. And some went on the floor. There,
*Timmy **don't** lick that.'*

'Oh, every baby is different,' said Aunt Fanny. 'You should
cling on to these moments, you know; they'll be gone so
soon . . .'

'Do you want her, then?' asked Julian, holding Lily out.
Fanny laughed. She seemed to have become possessed by a
spirit of jolly nostalgia that rendered her entirely impervious
to sarcasm, or the reality of the fears and doubts of their new
parenthood. About five minutes into their conversation, Julian

noticed that, no matter what he said, she always replied with advice.

'How old is she? Six months? You should really start feeding her proper food around now. *That* makes a difference to nappy changing, let me tell you. Ho, ho! Have you taken her swimming? That's a great way to meet other parents. Share war stories, and so on.' She chuckled again in that indulgent way that was really getting under their skin.

'Oh, you'll miss this stage, really you will,' said Aunt Fanny, unaware how close, in saying these words, she came to risking her own life. 'They're so nice at this age. Just you wait till she starts teething. *Just you wait.*'

'It seems to me like you're doing fine,' said Wendy.

'We're doing *what*?' said Julian.

'Just fine. Nice tea, this. Where did you get it?'

'Never mind that,' said George. 'Did you not hear a word we said? We're clueless. We are terrified all the time that we're going to do something awful by mistake. It's not right. This should be done by *professionals*!'

'Exactly what all good first-time parents think,' said Wendy, pouring a second sugar into her tea and stirring it. 'I haven't had fruit shortbread biscuits since I don't know when. They remind me of school. No – don't you see? It's the burden of good parents to think they're getting it wrong. If you thought you were doing A-okay, you'd probably be screwing it up in some major way. Excuse my language, poppet,' she said, kissing her finger and touching Lily on the nose with it. Lily, for her part, had shut up screaming when the doorbell rang announcing Wendy's appearance and had behaved like an angel ever since. 'Believe me, in my job, I get to see people not getting it right.'

Hearing Wendy was coming over had provoked mixed feelings. The housemates certainly didn't want Lily to be taken away. But they did want sympathy and understanding – approval, even. Their emotional demands on her were in fact strangely childlike.

But to be told that *this*, this trudging, illogical gulag they were in, was the way good parenting was supposed to be, well . . . well . . . When she'd gone their remarks stopped short of profanity, because they were good parents. But the overall message of Wendy's visit was hard to stomach: the prospect of this dreadful uncertainty becoming the norm, and continuing indefinitely. Nor, if truth be told, did they fundamentally trust someone who had two sugars in her tea.

'A sign of mental decrepitude,' Julian insisted. 'Coffee, I could understand. But not in tea.'

He looked over at his housemates, and discovered that

41

Lily had dropped off to sleep on Anne's lap, in the armchair, and that all the others had immediately followed suit, except Timmy, who was licking his hand in a bid for attention.

'Not now, Timmy,' he whispered. 'Uncle Julian's going to rest his head on the table for ten minutes . . .'

CHAPTER NINE

The Swimming Class

While Anne and Julian (and Timmy) were looking after the baby, George and Dick went out to buy a pram. They stood around in the department store, trying to catch the eye of a sales assistant, and looking over the products.

'That one,' said George. 'Baby fits in it; it's the cheapest pram. Let's go.'

'They're not called prams anymore,' said Dick. 'They're called buggies.'

'Actually,' said an assistant, sidling up, 'we call them travel systems.'

'Doesn't matter what you call it,' said George. 'We want that one.'

But shop assistants are like hypnotists. The more adamantly opposed you are to falling under their control (which George certainly was), the easier it is for them to get you. Within minutes, he was leading George and Dick up towards the pricier end of the aisle. They could not deny his logic that you get what you pay for, and he said he didn't want to see

43

them coming back in under a year because they saved money at the cost of durability.

'You will be with this machine day in, day out, for hours at a time. More than with your car, probably. You don't want one that's flimsy or tough to handle,' said the assistant.

'No,' said Dick. 'It doesn't bear thinking about.'

'And this one converts to a carrycot, you say?' asked George, chewing her lip as she looked one over. The assistant said yes, but it did lack the ability to clip into car seats, which many customers found frustrating. Now totally committed to finding the perfect buggy, George and Dick swarmed over the specimens in front of them, comparing notes. They examined puncture-proof tyres and limited-edition fabric designs, cup holders, dual-facing capability, lightweight magnesium-alloy frames, slim bases, bumper bars, air-sprung suspension and four-by-four all-terrain wheels, one-hand fold designs, jogging modes, rear wishbones, parasols and mosquito nets.

However, once Dick discovered the BabyCrooz Metro-Glider, he could not be shifted from it.

'It folds up *itself*,' he said, 'when you press this button.'

'Dick, I—'

'It has a phone charger, and running lights on the side!'

'Dick, we—'

'It's like one of those dreams where you find yourself on stage at the opera. Except it's real, and never-ending.'

'It has an LCD display that says how many steps you've taken and calories you've burnt! *We can't not buy this!*'

George turned to the assistant, who was looking totally impassive. 'Good job,' she said. 'Tell me how much it is.' He did so. There was a pause. 'Does it also have a Blu-ray player, or hovercraft functionality?' George asked. The assistant said it did not. 'It's just it seems to me that, for that price, it should. Do you accept IOUs, or donated kidneys? You don't. Okay, Dick – your funeral. You explain to Julian why this is on his credit card.' She sighed as Dick excitedly raced to the till.

The swimming class was on Wednesday morning, where Anne was delighted to be able to show off the new pram (even though she hadn't really worked out how to use it yet). George had point-blank refused to attend on the grounds that she hadn't worn a swimsuit in twenty years and she wasn't going to start now. (It was much too feminine.)

So, on Wednesday morning, Anne and Lily found themselves next to the pool in matching swimsuits (Lily with her swimming nappy underneath), and the class proceeded without controversy. There was lots of splashing and laughter, and much happiness, until one of the babies was sick in the pool, bringing the class to an end ten minutes early, which suited everyone except the pool cleaner.

In the changing rooms afterwards, Anne noticed there were two distinct groups of mums. First, the slightly posher set, who clearly took great pride in being pristine and having the most conspicuously expensive gear. And second, what Anne secretly thought were the less beautiful, but slightly nicer and more down-to-earth mums. She was very keen to speak to the latter group – although, as a boarding-school girl, she could probably pass in either. She just felt in desperate need for some advice from other mothers.

The friendly bunch all got on so well together (and were so used to being ignored by the posh mums, who perhaps Anne resembled), they didn't seem to notice she was there, trying to get to know some of them. While Anne was still struggling to dress baby Lily, which she was still far from proficient at, they all finished dressing and clattered out of the changing room in a loud, friendly bubble, presumably to disappear off somewhere together.

Anne turned instead to the posher mums, who were also gathering into a group.

'Hi,' she said to the nearest one of them.

'Hi,' said the woman blankly. Then she turned back to her friends and continued their conversation about how the nursery she'd taken 'little Xanthe' to had been the most expensive in the area, but had failed to get an Outstanding Ofsted report.

Anne watched and listened, fascinated and unsure for a moment what had just happened. She assumed that the nearest mum would be shocked, would rebuke her friend and introduce herself to Anne. After all, Anne was *right there* in front of them. Yet, to her amazement, the other women's eyes just flicked over her lazily, as though she were a cleaner, or a poster on the wall. They hadn't even noticed her.

'Come on, Lily,' said Anne in a husky voice, turning back to her. 'Let's get you in the pram.' She was moving like a robot, because these physical jobs had to be done, but she felt as though she'd been hit by a wall of emotion.

'Not since the playground,' said Anne to the others later. 'Not since the *playground* have I seen anything like it.'

'Let them try that on me,' said George. 'Let them just try it, and see if they like the consequences.'

'It was horrible,' said Anne, as she rocked Lily on her knee. 'I felt so stupid and ashamed. And I felt angry for Lily, as well. It was like they were rejecting her too. And no one should reject you, should they?' she asked her. 'No, they shouldn't. I could eat you up, little one.'

'Hey,' said Julian. 'It's Uncle Joodles' turn for a cuddle; stop hogging her. Yes, you like your Uncle Jules, don't you?' he said holding her over his head. 'Because he's firm but fair and intellectually rigorous, and one day he'll give you the short stories of Borges and the novels of Thackeray and you'll discuss them over an ale, won't you? *Yes, you will.* Yes, you will! Ha! She's laughing! Oh. Can someone pass me a clean muslin, please? Quick? Thank you. And some went on the floor. There. Timmy, *don't* lick that.'

CHAPTER TEN

A Consultation with Doctor Google

The following morning, when Lily had been crying almost all night, Anne began to fear she was sick.

'Are you sure?' asked Julian, peering close. 'I think she just *looks* sick – as anyone would – because she's been crying her face off for the past twelve hours.'

'Yes, but does she look sick because of the crying, or is the crying because of being sick?' asked Anne, worried.

'Well, OBVIOUSLY I have *no idea*,' screamed Julian, 'because I don't know how to bring up a baby! I mean, why are we doing this? Surely we should have had a few days of training, or something?'

'*Calm down*,' said George, slapping Julian once briskly across the face. She'd have liked to sock him one in the jaw, but that was just owing to her mental state and, in all fairness, he didn't have it coming. None of them had ever punched each other, although it was starting to feel like, if it was going to happen, this would be the scenario to cause it.

Their being in charge of a life seemed fundamentally wrong,

as though something had gone askew in the universe. But they were realizing now that this probably was something that all parents went through: from happy, arrogant youth into naked, trembling fear, an anguished rebirth at the hands of merciless and unpredictable fate. There was no fighting it, only meek acceptance.

These were the thoughts that went through their heads, albeit in a muddled sort of fashion, while George apologized for slapping him and Julian apologized for being hysterical, and Anne tried to examine Lily for symptoms. Timmy barked encouragement.

'Right, come on,' said George, opening her laptop. 'What do you think might be wrong with her?'

'Well, her face and neck are very red.'

George typed as Anne talked.

'Has she got a rash?' she asked.

'Nnnnnno,' said Anne. 'Although . . . Well, maybe the start of one. Also, she's very hot.'

'Is she having trouble breathing?'

'No. Apart from through her nose, which is blocked.'

'Have you noticed any irregularity in the stools?' George asked, pronouncing each syllable with doctorly precision.

'Well . . . no, I mean . . . how could I possibly—?'

'George, none of us has seen anything like what she leaves

'She has to sleep soon,' said Julian that night. 'If I cried that much I'd go into a coma.'

in her nappies in all our days,' said Julian. 'Could you self-edit the questions a bit, please?'

'Well, that's another symptom not to rule out, then,' said George.

'What do you think's wrong with her?'

'It could be anything. Could be respiratory syncytial virus. It's probably not that.'

'What's that?' asked Anne.

'It's very unlikely. I mean, symptoms would have to be much more advanced, anyway. What I definitely don't think it is, is meningitis.'

'*Meningitis*?' the other two shrieked.

'What's going on in here?' asked Dick, coming in sleepily from the other room.

'George is going on about Lily having meningitis!' said Anne.

'I'm not!' said George. 'Just take a breath. Everywhere I look online, I see symptoms that are the same as what Anne keeps saying. For instance, rubella. It starts like a cold, and then develops a rash . . . It seems we need to keep her away from anyone who's pregnant. Well, that's ironic.'

'She hasn't *got* a rash, George,' said Anne.

'Okay, okay. Has she got blue lips?'

'No, thank God.'

'Yellow skin?'

'What—? I mean, we've already discussed the fact she's as red as a tomato.'

'But that's because of the crying. Under that red, is she yellow? Because that could be jaundice.'

'Wouldn't that make her orange? No, I don't think she is. I mean, she can't be red and yellow, or red and blue, or all of them together at the same time, can she?'

George shrugged. 'I don't know.'

'Well, of *course* she can't. Her lips are normal colour, by the way.'

George reluctantly shrugged her acknowledgement, and kept reading. She ran her hand through her hair. 'Listen to this,' she said. '"My daughter was crying for several hours and I thought it was just normal baby crying, and then she went bright red, developed a rash on her neck and stopped breathing. We rushed her to A & E just in time and they managed to save her."'

'My Lord,' said Julian. 'What was the problem?'

'Actually, in this case, it turned out that she had swallowed some paint. So I don't suppose we have to worry about that so much. Why are you looking at me like that? Wait a minute. Listen to this: scarlet fever. Does her tongue have a white or yellowish coating?'

Anne looked miserably into the wailing baby's mouth. 'No, it's pink as anything.'

'Does she have a headache?'

Everyone watched George until she looked up from the computer screen.

'What?' she asked. 'Does she? She does? Oh, fine, I give

up. Oh, wait. Look at this. Has she had her nose blocked all night?'

'She might well have done,' said Anne. 'In fact, yes, I think she has.'

'Then the solution might be . . . Oh dear. Oh *dear*.'

'Out with it, George. What is it?' asked Julian.

'Oh, Julian, you're not going to like this one bit . . .' George said sorrowfully.

'I trod on a plastic toy swan,' said Julian.
'I think I'm bleeding!'

Julian came round and impatiently read the web page over her shoulder. His eyes widened in horror. 'But, no. But, oh, it's not *right* . . .'

'Well, what does it say?' said Anne. 'I can't bear the suspense!'

Julian, whose face had taken on a hardened look, just shook his head, refusing to explain.

'Stand back, Anne. I'll do this.'

She did, and Julian knelt down next to the squalling child. Anne watched in puzzlement as, very slowly, he lowered his mouth as though to kiss Lily. But as his lips reached her face, they fixed themselves instead over her tiny nostrils. Anne covered her mouth and looked away. But she failed to cover her ears and so she remained unprotected from what came next: a thin, whiny rasping noise as Julian sucked the matter from within Lily's nose that she did not have the strength to expel.

Julian turned away and let out an awful cry as he spat what he had just sucked from the baby's nostrils into a handkerchief.

'Aaaargh!' said Julian, scraping his tongue with his sleeve. 'I can't believe I did that.'

'But *look*,' whispered Anne. 'It's worked . . .'

Indeed it had, for baby Lily was now looking up at the

ceiling, in seeming astonishment and wonder that the thing that had been making her miserable was gone. Slowly, her eyes started to shut, and her tiredness caught up with her.

'We must none of us ever, *ever* talk about this,' said Julian solemnly.

CHAPTER ELEVEN

Relatives Bearing Gifts

Once they got used to their routines and Lily started to sleep, at least a bit, at night, life was by no means a walk in the park. It was *partly* a walk in the park, though, owing to all the walks in the park that they now had to take her on, in order to get her to sleep.

Aunt Fanny made another fleeting visit, leaving behind a cake (for which they were all enormously grateful) and a box of old toys she had stumbled across, which Dick turned out and rooted through nostalgically. There was a little wooden train set which ran on wooden rails, a wonderfully old-fashioned copper whistle and several little cars that had been carefully hand painted and put together with exquisite craftsmanship.

The housemates swooped on these old toys – the seemingly random wooden bricks that fitted together ingeniously to make an elephant, the toy snake that appeared to move of its own accord, the jigsaw puzzle where each piece was a wild animal of the jungle, but when you put it together, you had a map of Ceylon. All these old things filled them with nostalgia, and when Lily rose from her nap, they tried to engage her with them. They showed her how smoothly these handsomely planed and well-varnished blocks of wood fitted together – how well they cohered, aesthetically. She took one of the wooden blocks and rubbed its corner experimentally on her gums.

Seeing this, it suddenly occurred to Anne that after twenty years in an alternately damp and dusty attic, these wooden blocks might not be entirely hygienic. She jumped up to collect them and give them a quick wash in the sink and as she did so, her elbow caught a cardboard box that had been left on the kitchen table, sending it crashing down onto the floor. A large pile of brightly coloured plastic toys spilled onto the carpet.

'Oh rats,' said Anne. 'Where on earth did these come from?'

'Ah no, disaster!' said Julian, coming in. 'I wanted to throw those away before I got home, but I didn't have the chance. A colleague gave them to me – pressed them into my arms. What's the word …'

Anne bent down to put them back in the box. 'They really look . . .' she began. Cheap was the word that came to mind. '. . . new,' she said.

'Foisted, that's the word. He foisted them on me. Yes,' Julian agreed, helping her. 'They look all too new, in fact. Dodgy Cyril, he's called – he seems to have his hand in a lot of unsavoury pies.'

At the end of each shift, they switched. Except for occasional twenty-minute bouts of comatose exhaustion, Lily remained stubbornly and constantly awake.

'You mean, sweet pies? Or ones that have gone off?'

'No, Dick. I mean potentially incriminating pies.'

'Like the one in *Titus Andronicus*?'

'Just forget about the pies, Dick, I'm sorry I brought it up. I'm saying that knowing him, these toys came off the back of a lorry.'

'That's a silly place to keep a pie, isn't it, Lily?' Dick said, picking her up and kissing her. 'Actually, now I'm hungry . . .'

Anne and Julian quickly gathered up all the cheap toys: the TV-tie-in dolls, the cheap knock-offs, the pointless, weird, goofy gimmicks, the gaudy red plastic trucks, the yellow squishy animals, the glitter-covered pink squeaky things of every shape and size.

'Good gosh,' sighed Dick, as the final nasty piece of tat was placed back in the box, leaving only the handsome wooden toys laid out on the carpet. 'What sort of child *likes* that awful stuff?'

CHAPTER TWELVE

The Next Stage

'Why do I have to step on this horrible multicoloured crap *everywhere I go*?' yelled Julian, hopping.

'Wear slippers,' said Dick, without looking up from his iPhone and his bowl of porridge. 'It's everywhere. You know it's everywhere. Don't expect it not to be.' As he said this, he took a mouthful of porridge, his face creased and, pursing his lips, he ejected a red piece of Lego back on to his spoon, which he tapped on to the table.

Several weeks had passed and the collection of charming antique wooden toys, after being very briefly drooled over and used as teething aids, had been re-boxed and placed back in storage owing to neglect. Despite its dubious and possibly not entirely legal provenance, the very highly coloured plastic tat had now become a permanent part of their lives, their living room carpet and the colour palette of the flat. Baby Lily could no longer remember a world before it, and clearly did not want to.

It wasn't just the colours that were hard to live with. Many of these toys (not to mention the books that had been given and sent by friends and relatives) made exasperating noises. They weren't annoying the first or even, necessarily, the fiftieth time, but once a particular noise started to feel like it was going to continue forever, it began to drill into their psyches. There were toys that honked and squeaked and buzzed, made telephone noises, wailed the sirens of the emergency services and emitted monkey shrieks and duck quacks. This last made life complicated for Dick because his phone also made the sound of a duck quacking when people rang it, which led to many painful and fruitless dashes across the room before he thought to change his ringtone.

The flat had also undergone an involuntary redecoration. Mostly, it was the floors, carpets, furniture and the bottom few feet of wallpaper that had been daubed with handprints and food smears, thanks to Lily. But the others were responsible too, absent-mindedly putting down food-covered bibs and tea towels, or sicky muslins, or pooey nappies when trying to solve some other emergency, and then finding that those items had dropped, or spilled, or been trodden or sat upon. In the face of this, Anne had reached a realization with regard to her former compulsive cleanliness not unlike that of King Cnut's attitude towards the oncoming tide.

What was entertaining Lily this morning was a card book

'So this is our life now, is it?' asked George.

which played 'Here We Go Round the Mulberry Bush'. She pressed the button that played the song, and then pressed it again. Then she waited ten seconds before playing it again, and played it once more immediately afterwards. There followed the glorious eternity of a minute's quiet while she contemplated the ceiling, before she played it another ten times in a row.

'Right then,' said Julian, still massaging his foot. 'Ooh, is that coffee, Anne? You're a ruddy hero. I've shortened the list to ten.'

'Ten what?' said George.

'Top of my list is definitely flute,' said Anne.

'Ten *what*?' said George. 'You taking up instruments?'

'Not us, George,' said Julian distractedly. 'I'm minded to say saxophone, but I know you'll tell me it's too expensive.'

'What? *Her*?' said George.

'It's never too soon, George,' said Anne. 'You'd be amazed what they can pick up.'

'You could pick *her* up with a saxophone,' George said, pointing at the baby, who at that moment was lying on her side, staring at them intently and sucking her own foot. 'Dick? Back me up?'

Dick did not like being asked to pick sides. 'Well, she does seem, perhaps, a little young, it's true. But I suppose we can at least talk about it.'

Just talking was perfectly reasonable, but George insisted they concentrate on instruments that weren't larger than Lily would be at the age of one. They were quite happy, by the end, with a shortlist that included harmonica, bongos, ocarina, kalimba, ukulele, castanets and tin whistle.

'Although, if she keeps playing the ukulele into adult life, I shan't hide my disapproval,' said George. 'Everyone hates those guys.'

'Hey, what about a baby grand piano?' said Dick.

'They're not for babies, Dick,' said Anne. 'It's time for her bottle; can you sterilize one, please?'

The last few weeks of looking after Lily had not been any less tiring or frightening than the first few, but by now they were starting to wrench their lives towards a *routine* of tiredness and fright, where before those things had attacked them at random.

Anne had persevered with the swimming class, ignoring the 'rich bitches' and at last making friends with the other, more approachable mums. The only moment of awkwardness came when they were drinking coffee and discussing breastfeeding (during which Anne remained quiet), and one mother turned to her and asked, 'Don't you find that you always have one good boob and one dry boob?'

Anne was staggered and revolted by this, but, not wanting to

'Every baby is different,' said Aunt Fanny. 'You should cling
on to these moments, you know; they'll be gone so soon,'
she continued, unaware how close, in saying these words,
she came to risking her life.

get into explanations of Lily's complicated backstory, muttered awkwardly that, er, yes, she supposed she did.

In the leisure centre one day, Anne caught sight of the noticeboard and, on it, the extraordinary list of baby classes that were available. She took a picture on her phone and, when she got home, blew it up on her tablet to share it with the others – after all, Dick had promised that he and Julian would take Lily to a class.

'She could start to learn French,' said Anne excitedly.

'Look at this one. Baby massage. Is she *giving* the massage, or receiving it?'

They all thought about that for a second.

'Receiving it,' they all said.

'Baby gym,' said Dick, peering at the screen. 'Lots of names signed up for that one.'

'Oh, I wouldn't like to think of her losing her shape and getting out of proportion,' said Anne.

'I'm not sure they'd actually be pumping iron, as such,' suggested Julian.

'And I don't like to think of her up on those hoops either.'

Dick saw a satirical gleam in the look exchanged between George and Julian. 'Let's forget that one, then,' he said hurriedly. 'What else? Hmm. Not so sure about a cranial osteopathy class. Hey, look – baby karate. That would be hilarious.'

'She'd certainly look very pretty in the little white dressing gowns they wear.'

'But do babies *really* need to know self-defence?' asked Julian.

'Oh, look! There's a dads' group that meets in the park on a Friday afternoon. That's a wonderful idea for Julian and Dick, don't you think?' asked Anne. 'You can take Lily for some fresh air, get some exercise yourselves and meet up with other dads.'

Julian and Dick looked at each other. 'I'm game,' said Dick.

'What do you think the dads actually do?' asked Julian. He was making a mental exploration of the park to try and remember if there were any pubs or pub gardens that gave on to it. He assumed that some form of alcohol consumption must be involved.

'Oh, you know. I'm sure they just meet up and go for a nice walk, and have a bit of a gossip,' said Anne.

George looked at her quizzically. 'You don't know much about men, do you, Anne? No, I'll be intrigued to see how you guys report back. You could take Timmy.'

'Woof!' Timmy said, delighted. It was the first time someone had mentioned his name in weeks.

CHAPTER THIRTEEN

The First Rule About Dads' Club

Dick and Julian reached the park pretty much on time. They accomplished this by leaving forty-five minutes early. First, it took ten minutes for them to manoeuvre the buggy downstairs, then, when they reached the corner of the street, they had a brief argument about who had forgotten to bring the change of clothes and spare bottle. Losing the argument despite the fact he knew he was right, Dick nipped back for these and then they made good time until they noticed Lily's crying had turned to screaming. It seemed she had dropped Sophie the Giraffe at some point on the journey. Dick volunteered to retrace their steps, knowing that he would make a quicker job of it, but nevertheless, when he returned with Sophie in hand, Julian and Lily seemed frustrated by the delay and made fractious by each other's company.

'It was on the pavement,' Dick explained. 'I bought a bottle of spring water to wash it with.' Julian grumbled that this was a disappointingly acceptable excuse and they went on, arriving at the park tired and right on time.

At first, they couldn't make anyone out, but soon they spotted a group of men all doing leg and arm stretches in one corner of the park. They approached cautiously and then saw a bank of parked buggies nearby, which encouraged them.

'Ah, we have some newcomers,' said a loud voice with an Australian accent. Towards them strode a man who made the tall and athletic Julian seem like a feeble adolescent. 'Nice to meet you guys; good to have some new blood round here.' He shook their hands with unnecessary brutality.

'I'm Rider,' he said.

'Rider?' asked Dick.

'That's it. And this is the little one, huh?'

'Yes, we're her guardians because her parents are in prison,' said Julian.

'We're not a gay couple,' said Dick.

Rider affected not to hear this and instead introduced them to the other assembled dads. One of them was an Aussie mate of his – a thin, ratty guy with a sly grin, whose baby lolled in its sling like it had been drugged. There were three rather gruff men called Dave and Mike and Dave, and a nervous, balding, bespectacled chap who smiled too much and said nothing, whose name they didn't catch.

'Okay, we'll start with once round the park, then, shall we?' said Rider.

They were in love. Everything had changed.
Timmy watched, panting, fascinated.

They set out at a brisk jog, some pushing prams, some with their babies on their backs.

Rider at once began to talk to Julian and Dick, ostensibly to welcome them into the group, but he seemed at all times to be pushing ahead of them, creating a certain tension in the conversation. It didn't help that he never removed his wraparound sunglasses, which gleamed menacingly whenever he turned to look at them.

'Taken her first step yet?' he asked.

'No, no. She's just coming up on seven months. That's a long way off.'

'Well,' Rider said, 'you'd be surprised. Little Passion got there at eight months.'

'I'm afraid I didn't catch what you said,' said Dick, slightly out of breath and trying to keep up. 'What's little Passion?'

'My daughter, mate. Nine months.'

'Ah, ah,' said Dick. Never known for his ability to multi-task, Dick was finding this very difficult to manage. The most important thing by far was that he make sure Lily, who was strapped into her buggy, was safe. She seemed to be jiggling around an awful lot as they bounced over the bumpy grass and he was frightened that, should they hit a single tree root or hidden rock, the whole buggy might turn over and she could be squashed or break her neck. However, he was also trying to keep up with this ever-faster-speeding Australian man and maintain a conversation as well. He was starting to sweat profusely.

He looked over his shoulder to see if there was any help to be got from Julian, but he was jogging along in grim silence with the others, already a good distance behind. Turning back to the accelerating Rider, Dick saw an opening in the conversation.

'We read about this meet-up on the noticeboard at the leisure centre,' he said, trembling with the effort not to pant.

'You two take her swimming a lot, then?'

'Well, my sister does – you see, we all look after her together because, as I said, Julian and I are not a cou—'

'You started doing the sign-language class yet?'

'Oh, her? No,' said Dick, distracted for the moment by the fact that the names Julian and Dick were, in fact, quite ideal for a gay couple. 'Not yet.'

'Best thing we ever did,' said Rider, accelerating into what seemed like a sprint. 'Hands down. For our baby, for our family. It's amazing. She tells me when she's hungry, says that she's angry or sad, or that she's grateful. It's been such a magical time.'

'Right,' puffed Dick, adjusting his sweaty palms on the handles of the buggy.

'But I'll tell you the best class you'll find on that board: mindfulness.'

'Baby mindfulness? I don't think I even know what the adult version is.'

'Tranquillity and peace of thought. Meditation. Inward spiritual healing.'

'How . . . ? But—'

'That little rascal keep you and Julian awake at night, Dick?'

'Oh, you know, maybe now and then. We're not a—'

'Since we've been doing mindfulness, she sleeps through the night. Like a dream. Literally! Ha, ha!'

'Yes, ha. Well, that's good. That sounds great.'

They had finally come to a stop in shade under some trees on the other side of the park and Dick was bent double, leaning heavily on the buggy, his chest on fire, sweat dripping from his chin. He took in air with deep, cascading gulps.

'Mindfulness course,' said Rider. 'I swear to it and so does little Passion. She's signing it to you right now. You missed it. Anyway, you do that course, you won't regret it, mate!'

He ended his sentence by slapping Dick's shoulder with what might perhaps have looked like an encouraging gesture to the casual passer-by, but up close made the sound of a leg of ham landing on an ice pond.

When the others in the group caught up (they had been about two hundred yards behind), Rider made a big deal about having slowed the session down so as to 'go easy on the newbies', while flashing the now sweat-soaked Dick an indulgent smile. As a group, they jogged gently back round the park and then, with a wave and a shout of 'Good session, guys! See you next week!' from Rider, everyone dispersed.

Dick couldn't remember hearing anyone other than Rider

speak at any time. He didn't think he'd be able to speak himself for about half an hour. Between gulps of breath, he stroked Lily's head and silently decided that dads' club was perhaps not for him.

CHAPTER FOURTEEN

The Catchment Area

Early the following morning, they were all together in the front room, drinking coffee and playing with Lily. Despite lack of sleep, she was in a good mood – at her most charming, in fact. She couldn't quite crawl yet, but she had mastered all the individual movements that were involved, without managing to make them work in tandem. They could tell it was just a matter of time before this experimentation resulted in the discovery of locomotion.

Anne brought up the subject of musical instruments again, to which George replied, 'Are we *really* going to put her down for music lessons? I thought that was a joke. Surely we might as well try to teach Timmy to make scrambled eggs?'

'Woof!' agreed Timmy.

'This isn't about musical instruments,' said Julian. 'It's about schools. You've no idea how competitive they are in London. We may already be too late for several of them.'

George spluttered, but Anne nodded her agreement. 'At St

'You started the baby sign-language class yet? Best thing we ever did. She tells me when she's hungry, angry, sad or grateful. It's been such a magical time.'

Jude's, eager parents take along ultrasounds to register their kids. Not that we could afford St Jude's.'

George was aghast. 'Are you serious?' she asked.

'If we want to be serious about bringing up Lily as well as we can, then yes,' said Julian. 'I'm only sorry it took me so long to think of it. We should have done this weeks ago.' He fanned out a bunch of prospectuses for London schools on the table in front of him.

'Now, I've been swotting up on these and I've got some opinions . . .' he began.

'Me too,' said Anne. 'You want us to go for Meadow Hill Primary?'

'Sounds nice enough,' said Dick.

Anne and Julian both burst out laughing. It really seemed to hit their funny spot, because, after their initial burst, they went on and on. Lily joined in with the hilarity, in fact, and everyone gathered round to coo at her, George picking her up on to her knee. 'Jolly good joke, wasn't it, Lily?' she said, kissing the top of her head and nibbling her ear. 'Very funny by Aunty Anne and Uncle Julian, the comedians. Next stop for them, the Hammersmith Apollo.'

Finally, the pair's mirth wore off, Anne sighing and wiping a tear from her eye. 'Oh, Dick, good one. Yes, if we really think Lily would rise to the top in the crack-dealing trade . . .'

'Or,' Julian went on, 'if she could detect the best place to hide a stash of Uzis in a lock-up garage. Why, then, of course Meadow Hill Primary would be the perfect place. No, Anne was joking. Meadow Hill is the physical manifestation of the proverbial school of hard knocks.'

'What about St Pulsipher's?' asked Anne.

'Reputation on the wane, fees too high.'

'Hmm. Sandywell Lane?'

'Great results,' Julian conceded, 'but the only way on to the waiting list is if a family member went there.'

Anne whistled. 'Okay, give me your top choices.'

'My list of big hitters coming up. Number one: Rockwell Grange?'

'Very good, but out of catchment.'

'St Bede's?'

'My number-one choice. Out of catchment.'

'Horswell St David's?'

'Excellent; expensive; out of catchment.'

This suffices to give a sense of the conversation that continued in the same vein for the next forty-five minutes. Dick and George took Lily out in the buggy (to a park in the opposite direction of where they might run into Rider) and, when they got back, Anne and Julian had come up with a Plan. They outlined it while Dick sterilized some bottles and George changed Lily's nappy.

'There's no time to lose,' said Julian, looking at his watch. 'We've all got lots to do. We should move at once.'

'Locked and loaded,' said George, holding up a freshly changed Lily and handing her over to Anne. 'Dick, get the car keys.'

George and Dick were outside the estate agent's in fifteen minutes, having rung ahead to ask someone to show them all the available properties. When they pulled up, they saw a smug-looking young man in a cheap suit, clutching a folder and some keys, and smoking a Benson and Hedges.

'That looks like him,' said Dick.

George grunted. 'Let's keep this as brief as possible . . .'

Anne and Julian, meanwhile, were engaged on an entirely more complex and delicate operation. Quite against their character, they were about to undertake a deliberate piece of subterfuge.

Just like Dick with the BabyCrooz MetroGlider, they had become fixated upon St Anselm's Elementary as the only school for Lily. But getting her in would be no simple matter. When they looked up the school's website, they had been stunned to find today was an open day for prospective pupils, and they had phoned at once to book an appointment with the admissions officer.

They arrived just in time and received a tour around the wonderful facilities. They ogled at the board of past house and sports captains, who represented a cross-section of the country's most successful CEOs, athletes, film actors and rising politicians – male and female. They met the distinguished staff, who had exactly the air of courteous condescension Julian and Anne expected from public-school teachers. They were thrilled.

At last, they were invited in to meet the headmistress, a lavishly stern and humourless woman, and the admissions officer, a slightly crumpled middle-aged man in glasses. These two quizzed them on Lily's background and their ability to meet the fees (in response to which they handed over statements from their savings accounts). The subject of Lily's parenthood didn't arise (perhaps because Julian and Anne shared her surname), so they didn't mention it. They straightened their backs, spoke in their most cut-glass accents and, most importantly of all, tried not to appear too keen.

The headmistress and the admissions officer seemed impressed, and remarked that everything appeared to be in order.

*Despite having her own room, her cries were audible
from every corner of the flat.*

'There's one last thing, of course,' the headmistress said. 'I take it you are both practising Catholics?'

Julian saw Anne hesitate, and jumped in. 'Oh, yes,' he said, with his most confident smile. 'We love it.' His mind raced. Can't lose it now. So close.

'And do you attend out of duty, to try and get Lily into a good school, or do you actually live by the lessons of the faith?'

Sweet baby Jesus on a trampoline, Julian thought, she's laying it on a bit thick, isn't she? (Perhaps they *would* have to become Catholics, after all. He didn't relish breaking that one to George.) Perceiving that his robust confidence was not winning the audience over, he opted instead for humility.

'I don't feel we always get things right,' he said solemnly, 'but then that seems to be part of the territory, isn't it? But we try. That's why it's called "practising", perhaps.' He gave them both a wry and weary smile.

'Indeed,' Julian went on, warming to his theme, 'when we moved to the city, it was a wrench to leave behind our parish of St, ah . . . of St Botulph-upon-the-Marsh. Dear Father O'Grady will struggle without Anne to run the tombola at the summer fete. Won't he, Anne?' said Julian.

'Such a sweet man,' said Anne quietly. 'And I do so love his wife.'

'His *wife*?' asked the headmistress.

'Ha ha – just Anne's little joke,' laughed Julian, leaping up. 'I'm afraid you must have many more people to see and we don't want to take up any more of your time . . .'

'It's certainly nice to meet you,' the headmistress said as she walked them to the door, 'and we shall consider your application very closely.'

'I hope our prayers are answered,' said Julian, with a sickening smile.

CHAPTER FIFTEEN

Another Lovely Picnic

Lily was being rocked to sleep on Anne's shoulder when Dick and George returned, looking flustered but relieved.

'What's the result?' asked Julian tensely. 'Tell me you got something. You must have!'

'Maybe we did, and maybe we didn't,' said Dick mysteriously, walking to the window.

'You mean you did? Don't toy with me, Dick,' said Julian. 'In the past hour, I've been through an intensely humiliating process of religious impersonation. By the way, if anyone asks, we're all Catholic now. I've printed out the Wikipedia page and I'll give you the main bullet points later.' He passed out sheets of A4 to them all. 'Now, Dick, tell me you've found us a new abode and that we won't have to live above a kebab shop anymore?'

'Behold!' said Dick, waving his hand at the window. Julian and Anne crowded round.

'Where?' asked Anne.

'There. Over the road.'

Many of the toys made exasperating noises. Once a particular noise started to feel like it was going to continue forever, it began to drill into their psyches.

'You mean that flat, there? The one exactly opposite?'

Dick nodded. 'It seems the edge of the catchment area goes right down the middle of the high street. That flat was the only one available that was big enough, and in our price range.'

'But, Jesus Christ, it's above a *curry house*,' said Julian.

'Hey, watch your mouth – that's blasphemy,' said George, looking up from the printout. 'It says here that's a mortal sin for us Catholics. Don't you mean you're grateful to us for getting it sorted, Julian?' But Julian only responded with a grumble.

'Oh, Lord,' said Anne. 'I've just remembered – it's Saturday, isn't it? This afternoon is the birthday party Lily's been invited to.'

They all groaned at the prospect of getting dressed, leaving the house and talking to people.

'No, do let's go,' said Anne. 'If we tire her out at the party, she might sleep through . . .'

'Okay, I'm back on board,' said George. 'Where is this shindig?'

It was a party to celebrate the first birthday of one of the little girls from the swimming class. First birthday parties being more about the adults than the children, it was held in the pavilion of the local cricket club. There was a large, colourful picnic blanket and a shallow ball pool for the babies, and lots of nice people milling around and drinking glasses of punch.

'Booze?' asked Julian. 'I've almost forgotten what it is.' He left the group behind at once and went to the bar, hardly able to restrain himself while the barmaid finished serving the person next to him. Dick wasn't far behind. 'Please tell me that you have at least a small selection of British session ales.'

'I've got a nice IPA,' said the lady.

'A few weeks ago that would have been music to my ears,' said Julian. 'But things have changed. I am a new man. Session beer is my new happiness and desire: anything up to 4.2% alcohol by volume, *tops*.'

The barmaid seemed unsure if Julian was being serious, so Dick interjected, with a reassuring smile: 'We'll have two pints of this one, please. You see, we really need to keep it session.'

Within moments, two frothing pints of 3.8% ABV best beer were placed in front of them. Dick and Julian held them up to the sunlight to prolong this glorious moment of anticipation. Their hearts filled with wonder. Then they gulped, nervously at first, as though this could be some sort of sorcery. In unison, they set down the glasses and closed their eyes in exquisite bliss.

'Great parenting,' said George, arriving with a grizzly Lily in her arms.

'I'm off the clock, mate,' said Julian. 'Just stick her in the ball pool or something.'

'Come on, George,' said Dick gently. 'We haven't had a pint since the clocks went forward. It's now the cricket season. Don't spoil this very, very special moment.'

George retreated, muttering something about social services, until she found herself at the ball pool. Checking over her shoulder, she placed Lily down so that she could 'socialize' with her peers. Then, finding herself at a loose end, she returned to the bar and ordered a cider.

'DICK!' boomed an Australian voice from somewhere near the bar. Dick's blood turned cold, and he tried to wriggle away through the crowd, but he succeeded only in coming face to face with a beaming Rider. Glass of wine in hand and away from his exercise regimen, he seemed an altogether more relaxed and tolerable prospect. He gestured to a rather thin, nervous man beside him.

'I'd love to introduce you to my husband,' Rider said. 'Raymond, this is Dick; Dick, Raymond.'

'Ahh!' said Dick, shaking Raymond's hand enthusiastically. He felt a weight off his shoulders. 'It's so lovely to meet you . . .'

'Are we really going to put her down for music lessons? I
thought that was a joke. Surely we might as well try to teach
Timmy to make scrambled eggs?'

They all mingled. It was, after all, a beautifully sunny day and the cricket ground made for a picturesque setting, with the wind blowing through the trees and the smell of barbecue drifting over the crowd.

'I can't believe how amazing I feel,' said Julian, sitting next to Dick on the bench outside and handing him his second pint. 'Shame there's no game on, though.'

Dick agreed.

The people at the party were varied, interesting, approachable and pleasant. Anne, George, Julian and Dick found themselves sharing stories of the difficulties of parenthood, mightily relieved to find every single one of their fears and horrors were shared with others. Their confessions of parental failure drew, not shocked gasps, but laughter and reassurance.

Thus, over the course of a couple of hours, that afternoon there began to seep into all four of the housemates a feeling that this parenting situation might – *might* – not be impossible. And that they might – they may, *conceivably* – not be terrible at it. They seemed, if anything, to be exactly average and no worse than most.

They drank beer and ate cake, and laughed and chatted, more at peace with the world than they had been since that morning, months ago, when Lily had come into their lives.

Then they meandered to their separate cars (all five plus baby paraphernalia not fitting into one vehicle) and the two girls drove them home. Something approaching satisfaction and happiness had settled on them all.

CHAPTER SIXTEEN

Another Terrible Surprise

The car containing Anne and Julian reached home first, and while Julian divested it (slightly woozily) of the baby gear, Anne let herself in.

As she pulled her keys out of the door, she saw someone sitting in the living room and she screamed. Julian ran up the stairs and threw down the box he was carrying.

'Who? What? Who? Who is it?' he said, looking around.

Anne just pointed.

'Oh my LORD,' said Julian. 'What the devil are you doing here?'

'I'm afraid I've got some bad news,' said Cousin Rupert, from the armchair.

'*You've escaped from prison,*' breathed Anne.

'Indeed I have, but not in the way you're thinking. I used a lawyer. No rope ladder for me; I climbed out on a technicality.'

'You can't have her!' said Anne.

'You're right,' said Rupert. 'Not today, because her mother is still behind bars. But I wanted to let you know that we're

94

They were realizing now that this probably was something that all parents went through: from happy, arrogant youth to naked, trembling fear, an anguished rebirth at the hands of merciless and unpredictable fate.

going to start the formal process so that she can come home and be with her parents . . .'

'But – but – you *can't*!' said Anne. She had already started to cry, but she wasn't going, in any way, to allow that to staunch her fury. Julian moved protectively behind her, and put his hands on her shoulders. 'We're better parents for her. We've loved her more. We've . . . we've got used to her and . . .'

Rupert did not look impressed. 'I'm very grateful for the service you've provided while her mother and I were indisposed – truly I am. (Despite the fact that was a situation caused by you.) But once both her parents are free – you have to understand, we will want to be reunited with our daughter.'

'You'll just end up in prison again because of one of your schemes. And look at you – you don't care about anyone but yourself. Everyone knows that! We *cared* for her and *nurtured* her and you'll never be a tenth of the parents that we were to her! I'll prove it to social services!'

'What's all this fuss?' came Dick's voice up the stairwell. Shortly, both he and George appeared and looked suitably taken aback by their guest. 'Look who we found on the way up,' they said, and Wendy came in after them. She saw Rupert, and realized the bad news she had come to break gently to Anne, had arrived ahead of her. She stood in the doorway, looking sorrowfully at the weeping Anne, lost for words.

'I'm sorry, Anne,' said Wendy. 'I'm incredibly sorry. But this is the way it's got to be.'

'I'm going to lodge a formal application for custody,' said Anne. 'We've proved that we're good parents.'

'That's as may be,' said Rupert, standing and putting on his coat. 'I'll leave now. But at least you could let me see her.'

Anne suddenly stopped sobbing when she saw George's arms were empty. 'You haven't left her in the car?' she gasped.

'Of course I haven't,' George said. 'She's with you!'

'She's *not* with us,' said Julian. 'Dick, I distinctly said to you to fetch her from the ball pit!'

'No, you didn't,' said Dick hotly. 'You said *you* were going to fetch her from the ball pit.'

Anne screamed.

'So where, roughly, within the metropolitan area,' asked Rupert, 'is my daughter?'

CHAPTER SEVENTEEN

Bad Parents

They made their way back to the cricket club at top speed. All the way, the four housemates suffered an awful mixture of unpleasant emotions they would not wish on anyone. They felt panic that Lily would not be there. They felt stupid and ashamed for returning to the party like this. They felt humiliated in front of Rupert and Wendy. But most of all they felt a great gulping emptiness at the prospect of losing Lily.

Julian and Dick both secretly blamed each other, while the girls blamed them both equally.

At the cricket ground, they tumbled out of their cars and sprinted to the party, which – thank heavens – was still going on. They rushed through the remaining guests until they caught sight of the ball pen – and, in it, baby Lily, playing as happily as though they'd never left. She gurgled at the sight of them, and smiled her gummy smile.

Anne picked her up and squeezed her. She kissed her neck and head until Lily started to cry to get back in the pen. Anne

'She could start to learn French,' said Anne excitedly.
'Or baby massage.'
'Is she giving the massage, or receiving it?'

was crying again, as were Dick and Julian. George was looking hollow-eyed, stroking Lily's head.

Anne was dabbing her eyes as she put Lily into Rupert's arms. Anne couldn't deny that his usually serpent-like eyes flashed with something resembling human emotion as Lily rested on his shoulder and dribbled on to his expensive suit. Wendy, watching from nearby, noticed it too.

For her part, Lily took to him like he'd never been away, and threw her arms round his neck. It was this sight, of father and daughter together so naturally, that they would think of in the coming weeks and months, and that would make it easier for them all to give her up.

'I really *am* grateful,' Rupert said, rubbing his daughter's back. 'Really. And I don't want to make this any harder for you. After she's back with us, you can visit as often as you like, okay?'

Dick and George nodded, as Julian comforted Anne. It seemed only fair for Rupert to be given a short while to reconnect with his beautiful daughter, and they even heard him fondly mutter some baby speak as he strolled away to make a gentle circuit of the cricket pitch. Wendy followed a few paces behind him, to ensure he would actually return her.

'By the way, she's on solids these days, mate,' called Julian, 'so look forward to the nappy changes! Hah. That told him.'

They all subsided into deck chairs, physically and emotionally exhausted.

'Well, if there's one thing I can say,' said Dick, looking out over the people still enjoying themselves and chatting, eating and drinking in the sunshine, 'it's been no picnic.'

'He means our situation,' said George, to someone nearby who looked over, 'not this. This *is* a picnic. He didn't mean the picnic. He meant the thing that's specifically *not* been . . . It doesn't matter.'

They all lay in the chairs, silently zonked out for a few moments, listening to the wind in the trees, before they heard a noise they recognized. One by one, they sat up. They looked at each other.

'TIMMY!' said Anne.

Hearing her voice, Timmy bounded over. 'Woof!' he said. 'Woof, woof!'

He was overjoyed to see them, and especially to be lavished with the adoration and attention which they now poured on him, and which he had sought for in vain in the many preceding weeks.

'Oh, Timmy, what *terrible* parents we've been,' said Dick, ruffling his fur. 'We managed to not leave just one child here, but two!'

'Woof!' said Timmy happily, showing that all was forgiven.

'We are terrified all the time. It's not right.
*This should be done by **professionals**.'*

Like Lily, he had been having a wonderful time at the party. Unlike Lily, he had been enjoying some amorous adventures in the cemetery behind the club house with a coquettish bassett hound. As long as everyone was happy with him, he was more than happy with them.

'Timmy, just you wait until we get you home. We're going to move your basket back to pride of place in the kitchen, and out of that horrible cupboard, and then we're going to get you some lovely wet food that you like and, tomorrow, take you on the longest walk of your life and throw you a thousand sticks! We'll be the best parents to you that a dog ever had!'

'Woof!' said Timmy. 'Woof! Woof!'